Who's Bad
and Who's Good,
Little Red
Riding Hood?

Written by Steve Smallman

Illustrated by Neil Price

Once upon a time
there was a girl called
Little Red Riding Hood.

It wasn't her real name – it was just what
everyone called her because she was little and
always wore a red cloak with a hood.

This book belongs to:

· · · · · · · · · · · · · · · · · · · ·

· · · · · · · · · · · · · · · · · · · ·

Quarto is the authority on a wide range of topics.

Quarto educates, entertains and enriches the lives of our readers—enthusiasts and lovers of hands-on living. www.quartoknows.com

Editor: Joanna McInerney
Designer: Chris Fraser
Series Designer: Victoria Kimonidou
Publisher: Maxime Boucknooghe

© 2017 Quarto Publishing plc

First Published in 2017 by QED Publishing,
an imprint of The Quarto Group.
The Old Brewery, 6 Blundell Street,
London N7 9BH, United Kingdom.
T (0)20 7700 6700 F (0)20 7700 8066
www.QuartoKnows.com

A catalogue record for this book is available from the British Library.

ISBN 978 1 78493 957 1

Manufactured in Huizhou, China TL102017

9 8 7 6 5 4 3 2 1

One day, her mum asked her to take some cupcakes
and soup to her grandma who lived in the woods.

"Stick to the path
and don't talk to
strangers!" said
her mum. "And
if you do meet a
stranger, yell,
run and tell!"

"Who should I tell?" asked Little Red Riding Hood.

"Someone you know or a policeman
or a person in a shop," replied her mum.

On the way to Grandma's house
Little Red Riding Hood heard
someone coughing behind a tree.

It was a wolf!

"Hello, what are you doing out here all by yourself?" he croaked.

"A stranger!" gasped Little Red Riding Hood.

"I'M GOING TO GRANDMA'S HOUSE SO LEAVE ME ALONE!" she yelled.

She ran and ran until she met...

...a rabbit.

"Oh, hello, what's wrong?" asked Rabbit.

"I'm on my way to Grandma's house with some cakes and soup and I saw a big bad wolf, but I yelled and ran away!" gabbled Little Red Riding Hood.

"Oh dear, how awful!" said Rabbit.
"Why don't you pick some flowers for
your dear grandma, then I'll come
with you to keep you safe."

"Oh thank you!" said Little Red
Riding Hood, "That would be lovely!"

While Little Red Riding Hood picked flowers,
she told Rabbit all about her grandma.

"She's very old and she still lives by herself.
Mum says it's not safe for her to be all alone,
especially when she's got so much jewellery!"

"I can't wait to
meet her!" said Rabbit.

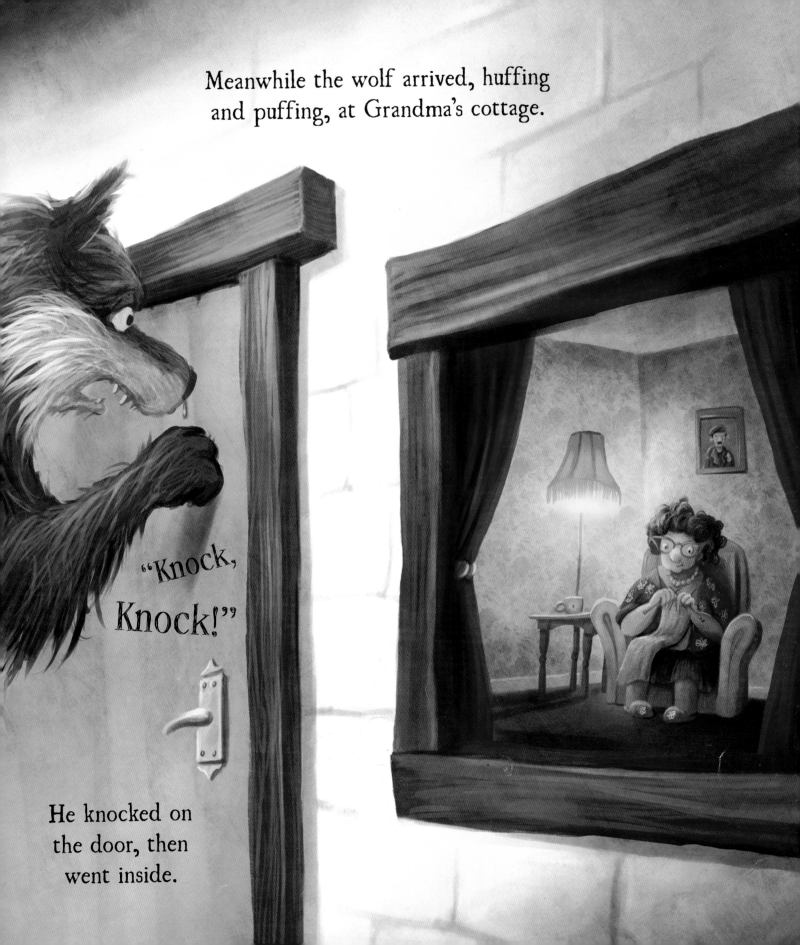

Meanwhile the wolf arrived, huffing
and puffing, at Grandma's cottage.

"Knock,
Knock!"

He knocked on
the door, then
went inside.

When Little Red Riding Hood arrived at
the cottage, she found someone snuggled up in
Grandma's bed wearing a nightie and cap.

"Oh Grandma, what
big eyes you have!"
said Little Red
Riding Hood.

"Well they must work better than yours!"
replied the wolf, "I'm not your grandma!"

"Yes dear?" replied Grandma,
walking into the room carrying a tea tray.
"What on earth is the matter?"

"Oh! I thought this big
bad wolf had eaten you!"
cried Little Red Riding Hood.

"I didn't!"
croaked the wolf.

"He was about to!"
cried Rabbit moving
towards the door.

But just then...

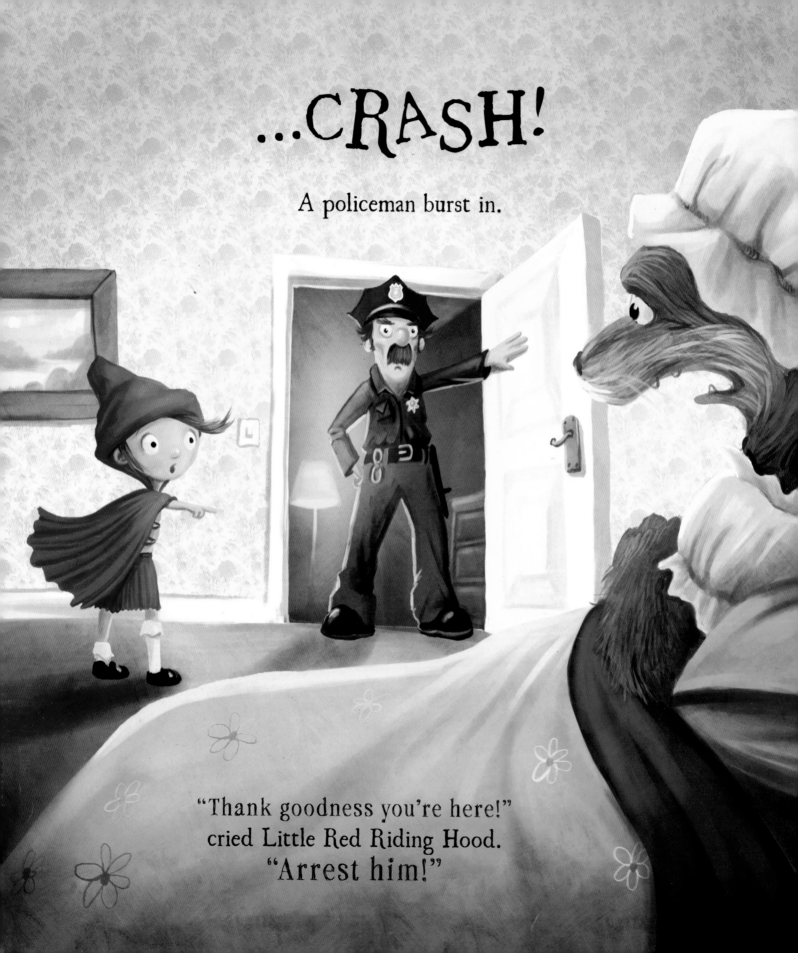

"I will!" said the policeman...

...and he grabbed the
rabbit by the ears.

"Will someone please tell me what is going
on here?" shouted Little Red Riding Hood.

So Grandma told her...

"Mr Wolf is a friend of mine. He came to warn me that you were all alone in the woods and that you were talking to strangers. So we called the police."

"Mr Wolf looked poorly when he got here so I made him put on something warm and get into bed. Then I made some tea."

"So that's why you're wearing
Grandma's nightie and cap!"
said Little Red Riding Hood.

"Yes," replied Mr Wolf, "I might look
silly but I'm lovely and warm!"

"Even though you yelled and ran away, you told me where you were going. And you spoke to Rabbit, but you didn't know him either," said Mr Wolf.

"But he's really nice!"
argued Little Red Riding Hood.

"No he isn't," said the policeman. "This is the famous Bunny Burglar. We've been after him for ages."

The policeman tipped Rabbit's bag upside down and out fell Little Red Riding Hood's cupcakes, the soup, Grandma's jewellery and many things they'd never seen before!

The policeman led Rabbit away.

"I was so sure Rabbit was good and Wolf was bad," sighed Little Red Riding Hood.

"You can't always tell who's bad and who's good. Mr Wolf is lovely and now you know him, he's not a stranger." said Grandma.

Little Red Riding looked over at Mr Wolf
who was sitting in bed, drinking tea and still
wearing Grandma's nightie and cap.

"Well, he might not
be a stranger," giggled
Little Red Riding Hood,
"but he definitely
looks strange!"

Next steps

Show the children the cover again. When they first saw it, did they think that they already knew the story? How is this story different from the traditional story? Which parts are the same?

Little Red Riding Hood's mummy told her not to talk to strangers. Why do you think she said that? What did she tell Little Red Riding Hood to do if she did meet a stranger?

In the story, what did Little Red Riding Hood do when she met the wolf? Did she do the same thing when she met the rabbit? Why not?

Little Red Riding Hood thought that the wolf was bad and the rabbit was good. Was she right? Can you tell if somebody is good or bad just from the way they look?

Discuss with the children that a stranger is anyone that they do not know. They can be male, female, young or old. Ask the children what they think they should do if they meet a stranger.

Ask the children to draw a picture of the wolf looking very silly in Grandma's nightie and cap. Make sure to include the big eyes and sharp teeth!